WONDER BOOKS

Vets

The Sound of V

By Peg Ballard

The Child's World®, Inc.

The vet helps many pets.

V

OFFICE OPEN
7 DAYS A WEEK
8:30 AM
EMERGENCIES CALL
564-2660
EVENING & WEEKEND
HRS. BY APPT.
AAHA
AMERICAN
ANIMAL
HOSPITAL
ASSOCIATION

The vet helps the dog.

The vet helps the cat.

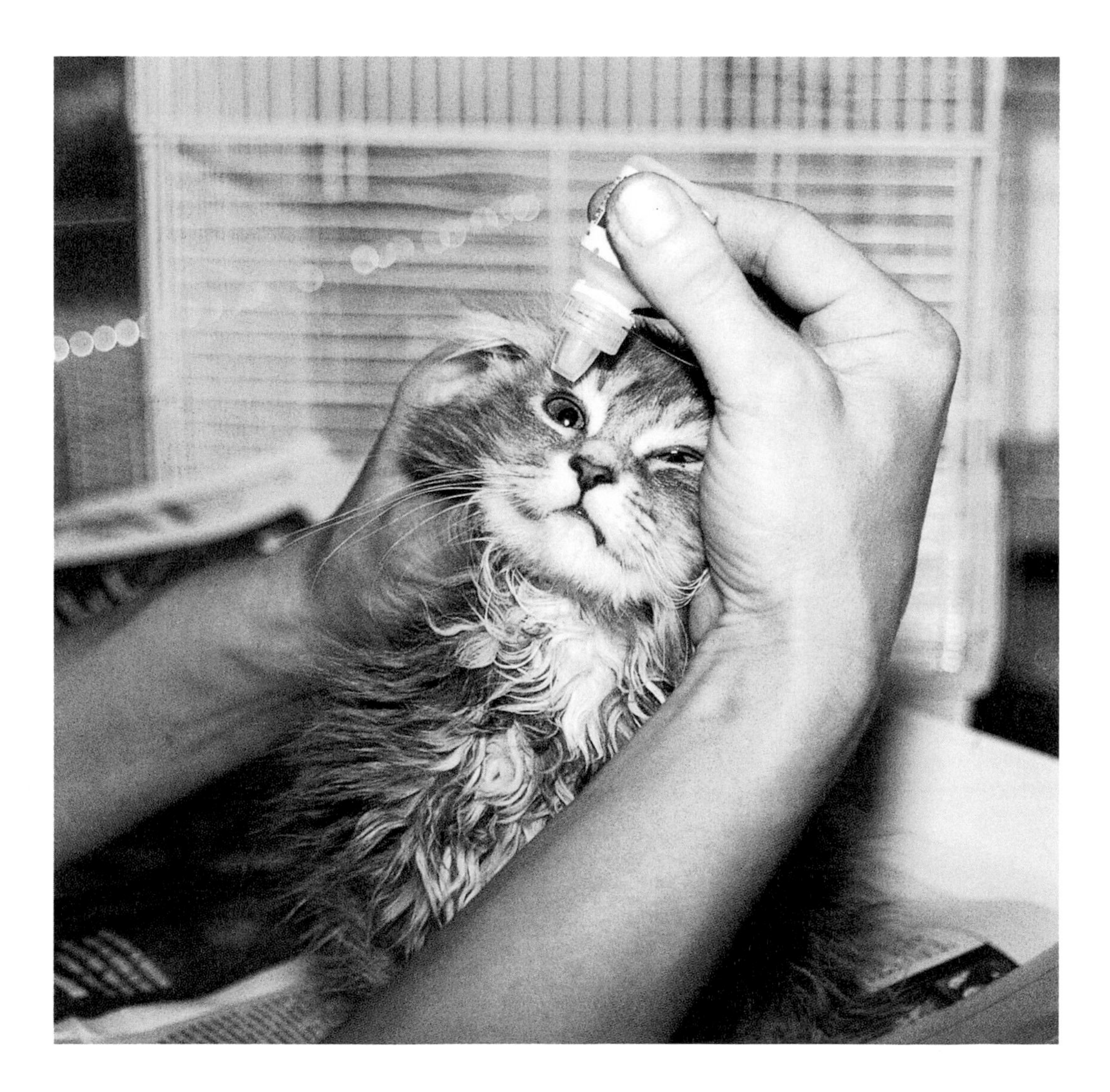

The vet helps the cow.

The vet helps the pony.

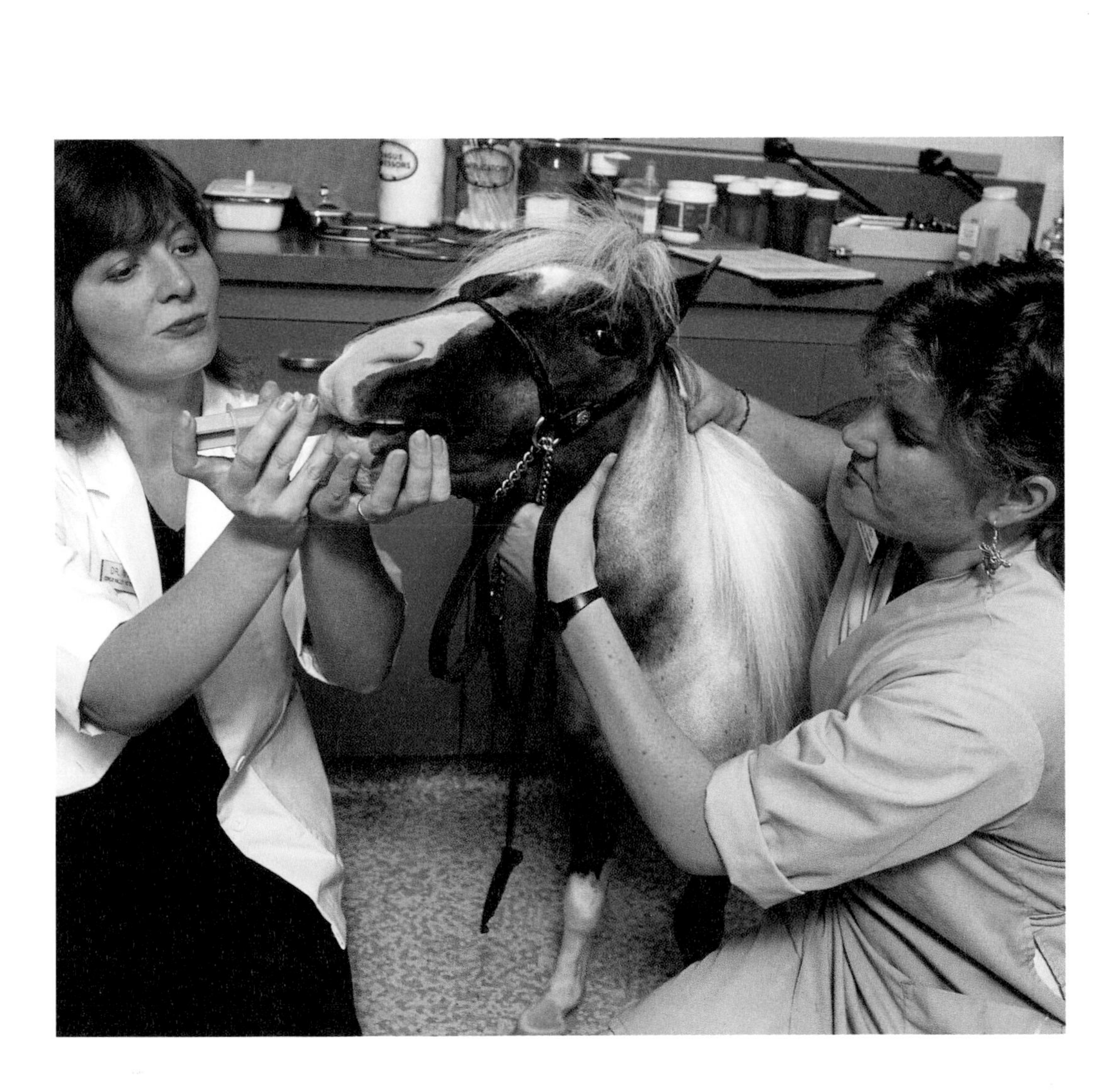

Some pets visit the vet.

Some vets visit the pet.

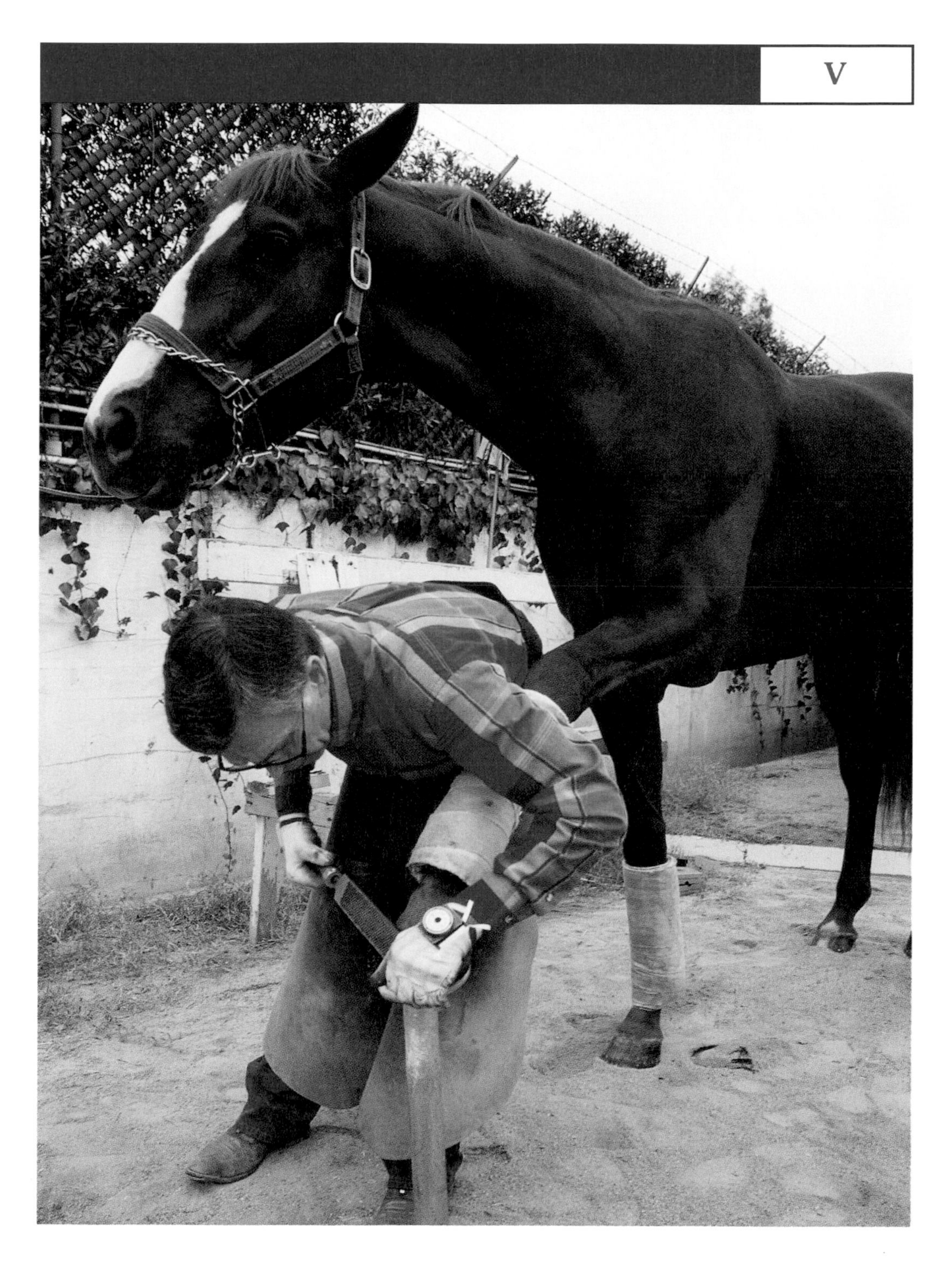

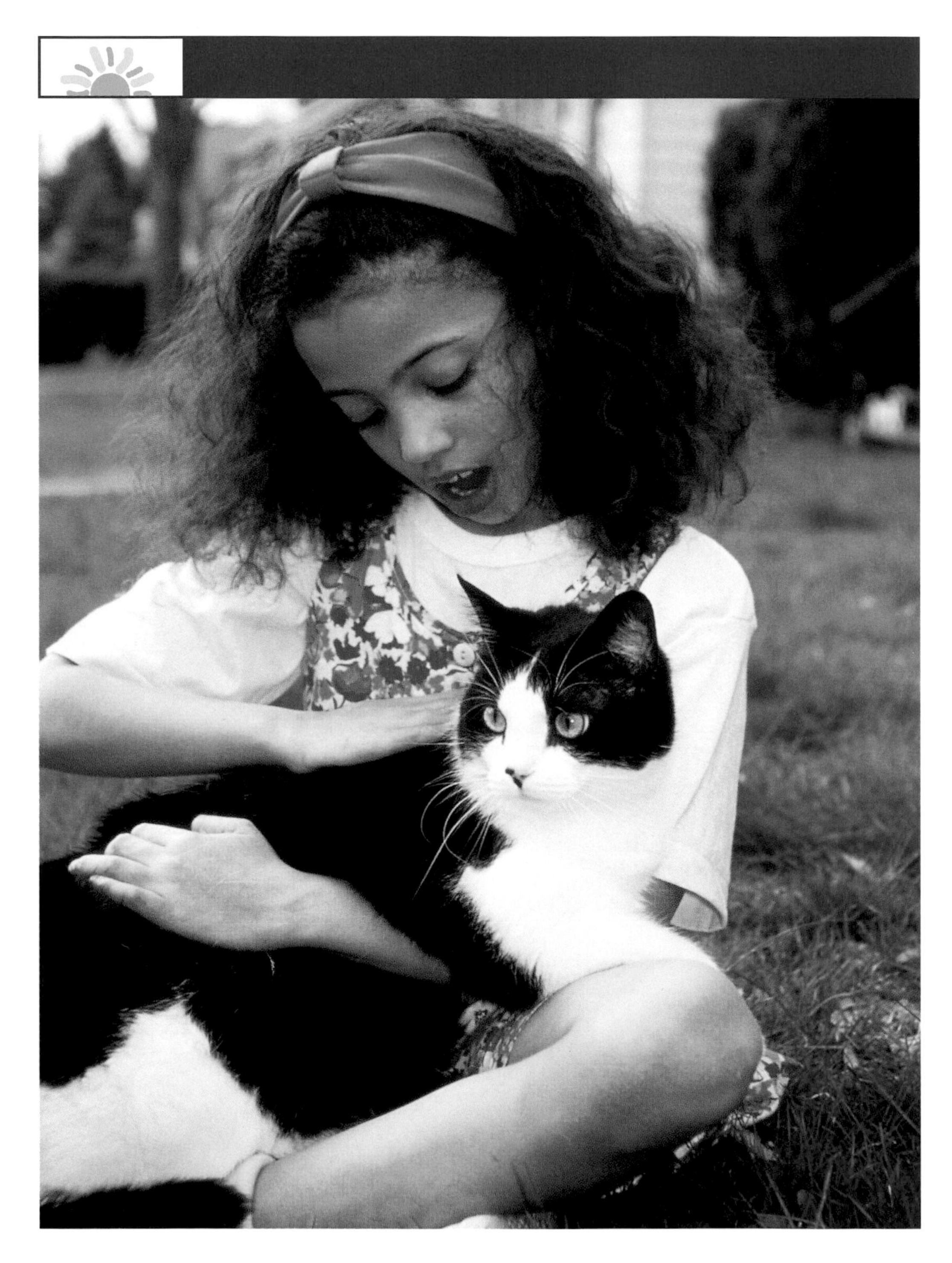

Val has a pet.

Val's sister takes her pet to the vet.

The vet helps Val’s pet.

Word List

Val

vet

visit

Note to Parents and Educators

The books in the Phonics series of the Wonder Books are based on current research which supports the idea that our brains are pattern detectors rather than rules appliers. This means children learn to read easier when they are taught the familiar spelling patterns found in English. As children encounter more complex words, they have greater success in figuring out these words by using the spelling patterns.

Throughout the 35 books, the texts provide the reader with the opportunity to practice and apply knowledge of the sounds in natural language. The 10 books on the long and short vowels introduce the sounds using familiar onsets and rimes, or spelling patterns, for reinforcement. For example, the word "cat" might be used to present the short "a" sound, with the letter "c" being the onset and "-at" being the rime. This approach provides practice and reinforcement of the short "a" sound, as there are many familiar words made with the "-at" rime.

The 21 consonants and the 4 blends ("ch," "sh," "th," and "wh") use many of these same rimes. The letter(s) before the vowel in a word are considered the onset. Changing the onset allows the consonant books in the series to maintain the practice and reinforcement of the rimes. The repeated use of a word or phrase reinforces the target sound.

The number on the spine of each book facilitates arranging the books in the order that children acquire each sound. The books can also be arranged into groups of long vowels, short vowels, consonants, and blends. All the books in each grouping have their numbers printed in the same color on the spine. The books can be grouped and regrouped easily and quickly, depending on the teacher's needs.

The stories and accompanying photographs in this series are based on time-honored concepts in children's literature: Well-written, engaging texts and colorful, high-quality photographs combine to produce books that children want to read again and again.

Dr. Peg Ballard
Minnesota State University, Mankato

Photo Credits

All photos © copyright: C. Osinski: 4; PhotoEdit: 15 (Bill Aron), 19 (Hutchings); Photri, Inc.: 8; Romie Flanagan/Flanagan Publishing Services: 7, 20; Tony Stone Images: 3 (Kathi Lamm), 12 (Zigy Kaluzny); Unicorn Stock Photos: 11 (A. Ramey), 16 (Jeff Greenberg/dMRp). Cover: Tony Stone/Kathi Lamm.

Photo Research: Alice Flanagan
Design and production: Herman Adler Design Group

Printed in the United States of America.

Library of Congress Cataloging-in-Publication Data

Ballard, Peg.
Vets : the sound of "v" / by Peg Ballard.
p. cm. — (Wonder books)
Summary : Simple text and repetition of the letter "v" help readers learn how to use this sound.
ISBN 1-56766-700-7 (lib. bdg. : alk. paper)
[1. Veterinarians Fiction. 2. Alphabet.] I. Title. II. Series: Wonder books (Chanhassen, Minn.)
PZ7.B21195Ve 1999
[E]—dc21 99-25549
CIP

P9-CFL-033

GEOGRAPHY FROM A TO Z

A PICTURE GLOSSARY

GEOGRAPHY FROM A TO Z

A PICTURE GLOSSARY

By Jack Knowlton Pictures by Harriett Barton

Thomas Y. Crowell New York

Geography from A to Z: A Picture Glossary

Printed in Singapore.
1 2 3 4 5 6 7 8 9 10

Library of Congress Cataloging-in-Publication Data
Knowlton, Jack.
Geography from A to Z: a picture glossary.

Summary: A glossary of geographic terms, from "archipelago" to "zones," with definitions and descriptions of the Earth's features.
1. Geography—Dictionaries, Juvenile. [1. Geography—Dictionaries] I. Barton, Harriett. II. Title.
G63.K63 1987 910'.3'21 86-4594
ISBN 0-690-04616-2
ISBN 0-690-04618-9 (lib. bdg.)

For our fathers
John C. Knowlton, Sr.
and
Byron A. Wyatt

Archipelago—a group of islands clustered together in an open expanse of sea or ocean. The Philippine Islands are a large archipelago.

OCEAN

LAGOON

Atoll—small tropical islands and reefs that encircle shallow pools of seawater called **lagoons**. Atolls and reefs are built of **coral**, the rocklike, compacted skeletons of billions upon billions of tiny sea animals called polyps.

Badland—rocky wasteland that has been carved by erosion into intricate and fantastic shapes. **Erosion** is the process by which water, wind, and ice slowly change the shape, size, and look of every feature on Earth by wearing it away.

Bay—a small area of sea or lake partly enclosed by dry land. **Coves** and **inlets** are very small bays. Some deep, sheltered bays are called **harbors**.

Beach—the sandy or rocky land at the edge of an ocean, sea, or lake. Beaches are part of the **coastline** or **seashore**.

Butte—an isolated, rocky hill or mountain with a *small* flat top. A **mesa** is similar to a butte except it has a *large* flat top.

Canyon—a deep, narrow valley with steep, rocky sides. Flowing along the bottom or **floor** of most canyons is the river that created it by carving through the surrounding rock. Small canyons are called **chasms**, **gorges**, or **ravines**.

Cape—a pointed piece of land that projects from a coastline. Small capes are often called **points** or **spits**.

Cave—a hollow underground chamber, usually one with an opening in the side of a hill or mountain. A **cavern** is a large cave or a series of connected caves.

Cliff—a sheer, steep face of rock or earth. A **bluff** is similar to a cliff but is less steep and has a broad, softly rounded face. A high, overhanging edge of a cliff is called a **precipice**.

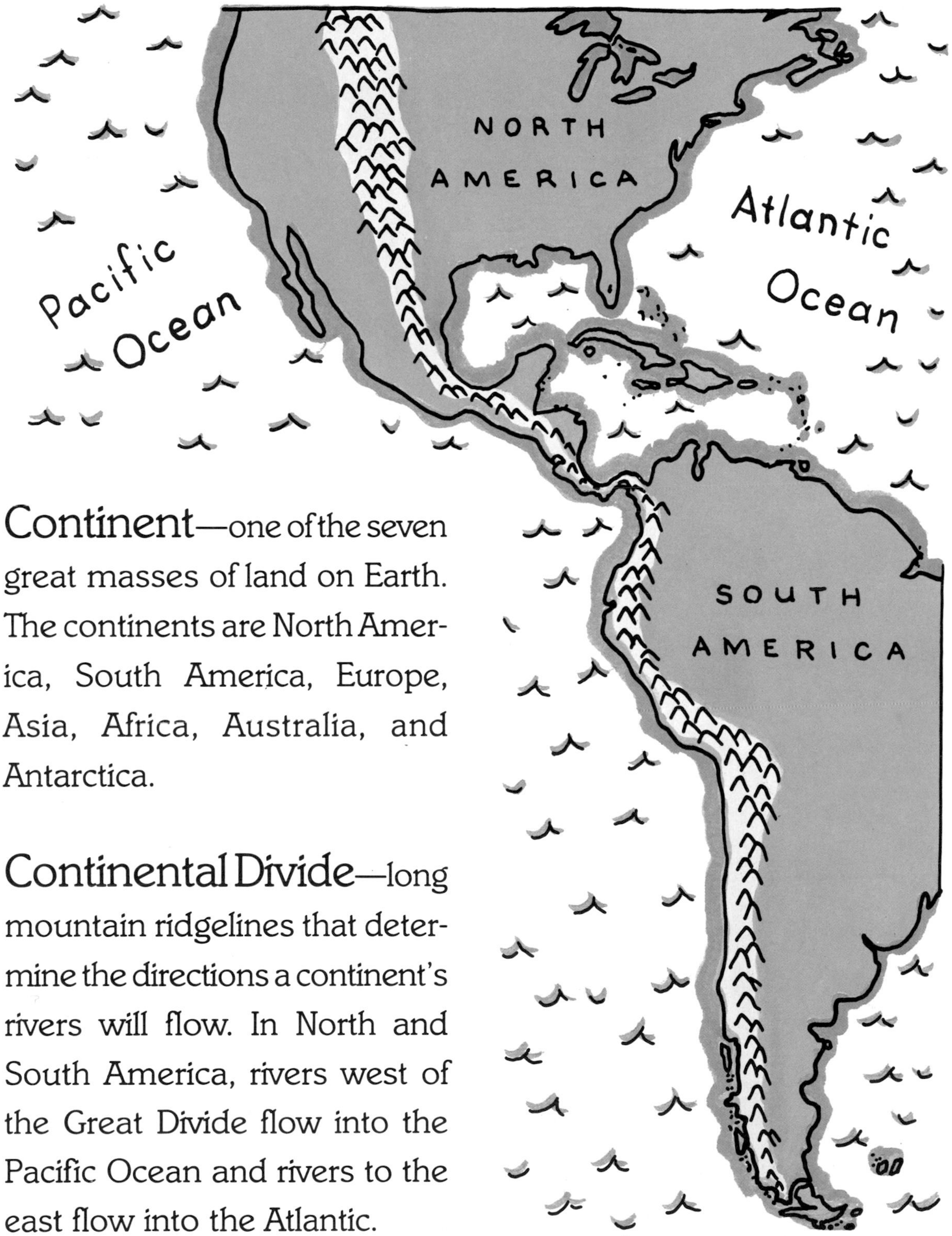

Continent—one of the seven great masses of land on Earth. The continents are North America, South America, Europe, Asia, Africa, Australia, and Antarctica.

Continental Divide—long mountain ridgelines that determine the directions a continent's rivers will flow. In North and South America, rivers west of the Great Divide flow into the Pacific Ocean and rivers to the east flow into the Atlantic.

Continental Shelf—a shallow underwater plain that is the real outer edge of a continent. The continental shelf ends at the **continental slope**, a cliff that plunges to the deep ocean floor.

Crevasse—a deep crack in either the ice on top of a glacier or the ground after an earthquake.

Delta—a fan-shaped deposit of mud and sand, often green with vegetation, found at the mouths of many rivers.

Desert—a very dry and desolate land that receives little or no rainfall. Most deserts are covered with rocks and stones. Only one fifth of all desert surfaces are covered with sand. An **oasis** is an isolated green spot in a desert where water flows up from an underground spring.

Dune—a mound or ridge of loose sand shaped by blowing winds. Dunes are found both in deserts and along seashores.

Fjord—a long, narrow inlet of the sea between tall, rocky cliffs.

Ford—a shallow place in a stream where people and animals can safely wade from one bank to the other.

Forest—a region thickly covered with trees and abundant underbrush. Forests are also called **woodlands** or **woods**.

Geyser—a very hot, or **geothermal**, spring that shoots scalding water and steam high into the air. In the Icelandic language the word *geyser* means "roaring gusher."

Glacier—a great mass of ice slowly sliding down a mountain slope or through a valley. Glaciers are very slowly moving rivers of ice.

Grassland—a vast open plain covered with natural or planted grasses. Tropical grasslands are called **savannas**. In other parts of the world grasslands have various names: **pampas**, **prairies**, **plains**, **veldts**, or **steppes**.

Gulch—a small, narrow, rocky ravine. Sometimes a violent mountain stream called a **torrent** races through a gulch. A **gully** is a jagged ditch gouged through dirt or clay by heavy rainstorms.

Gulf—a large inlet of ocean or sea that is partially surrounded by land. Gulfs are much bigger and deeper than bays.

Headwater or **Source**—the area where a river originates and begins its journey to the sea. Headwaters are regions rich in rainfall, melting snow, and bubbling springs. **Springs** are openings in the earth where underground water flows to the surface.

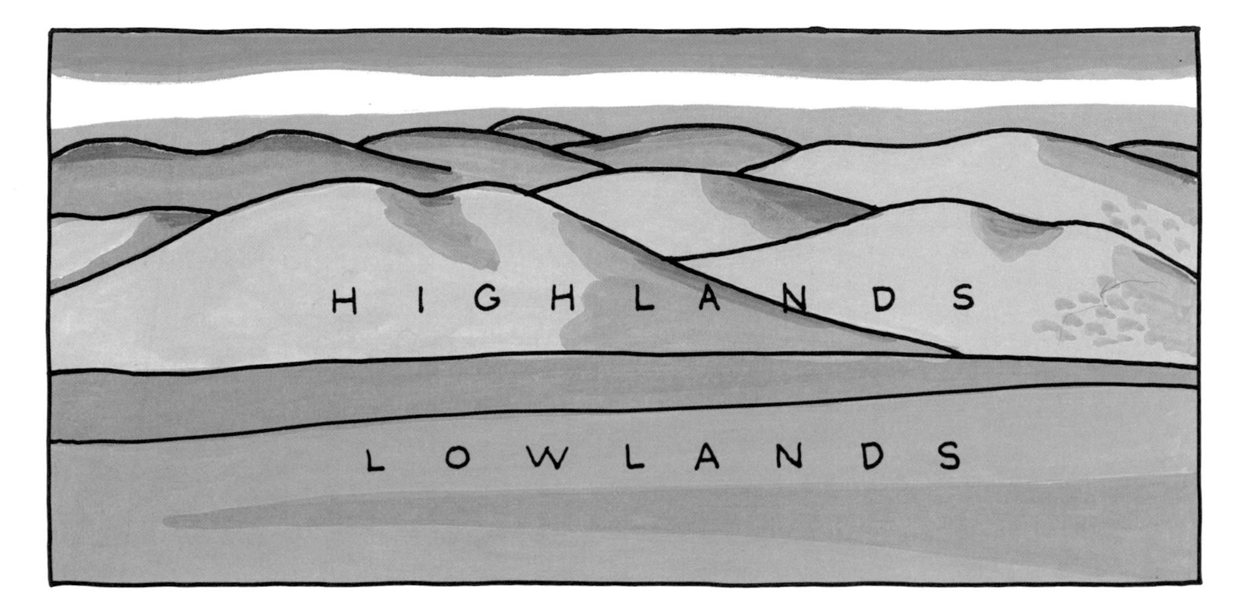

Highland—a mountainous or hilly region that stands above the surrounding landscape. A **lowland** is just the opposite—a low, flat area of land.

Hill—an elevated, rounded point of land that is lower and smaller than a mountain. A **knob** is a small hill; a **knoll** is even smaller.

Iceberg—a large chunk of floating ice that has broken off, or calved, from a glacier. Icebergs often break apart into smaller pieces called **bergs, bitty bergs,** or **growlers.** About nine tenths of an iceberg floats beneath the water.

Island—a piece of land that is smaller than a continent and completely surrounded by water. Very small islands are called **isles** and **islets**.

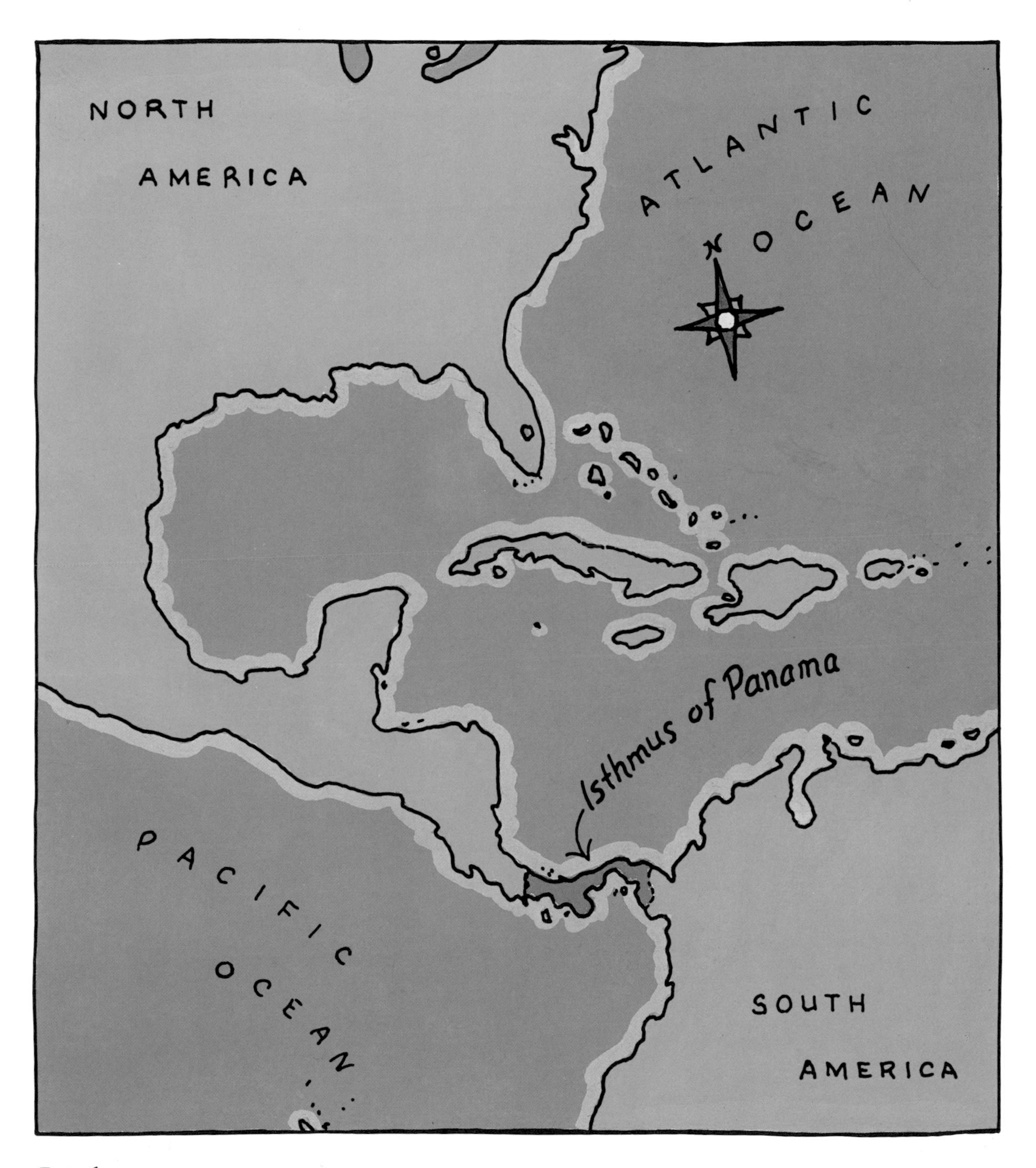

Isthmus—a narrow strip of land that does two things: (1) it connects two much larger areas of land, and (2) it narrowly separates two large bodies of water.

Jungle—a hot, humid, tropical rain forest. Most jungles are located near the equator.

Key—a very small, low, offshore island or reef. Keys are built from coral and sand.

Lake—a large inland body of water. Lakes are bigger than **ponds**, and ponds are bigger than **pools**.

Marsh—a low, spongy wetland covered with thick, healthy growths of tall grasses and reeds. A **bog** is a marsh filled with stagnant water and dead, decaying plants. Bogs are mostly found in northern climates.

Meander—a bend in the winding, looping course of many lowland rivers. Sometimes, the river channel will break through the narrow neck of a loop to create curved bits of water called **oxbow lakes**.

Mountain—a rugged, upthrust mass of rock that looms high above the surrounding land. Mountains are sometimes called **mounts**. Mountaintops have several names: **peaks**, **pinnacles**, **crests,** or **summits**.

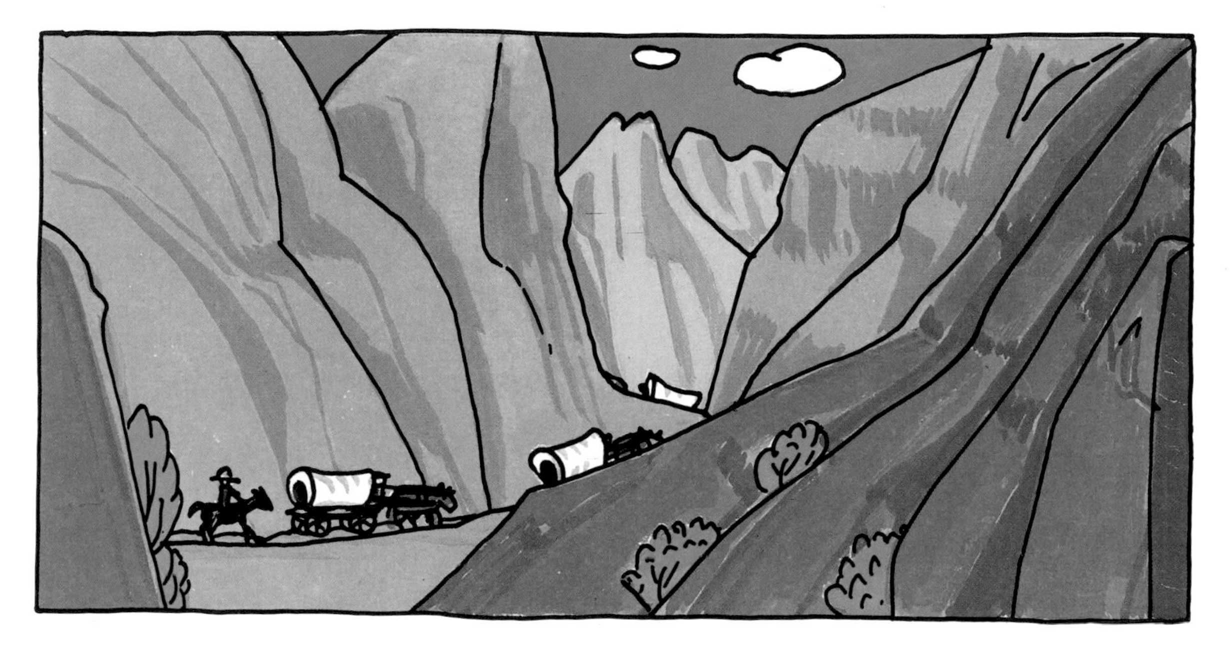

Mountain Pass—an opening or **gap** in a mountain range that serves as a path or road across the mountains.

Mountain Range—a long, connected chain of mountains and hills.

Mouth—the place where a stream flows into a larger body of water. The mouth of a river is the end of that river.

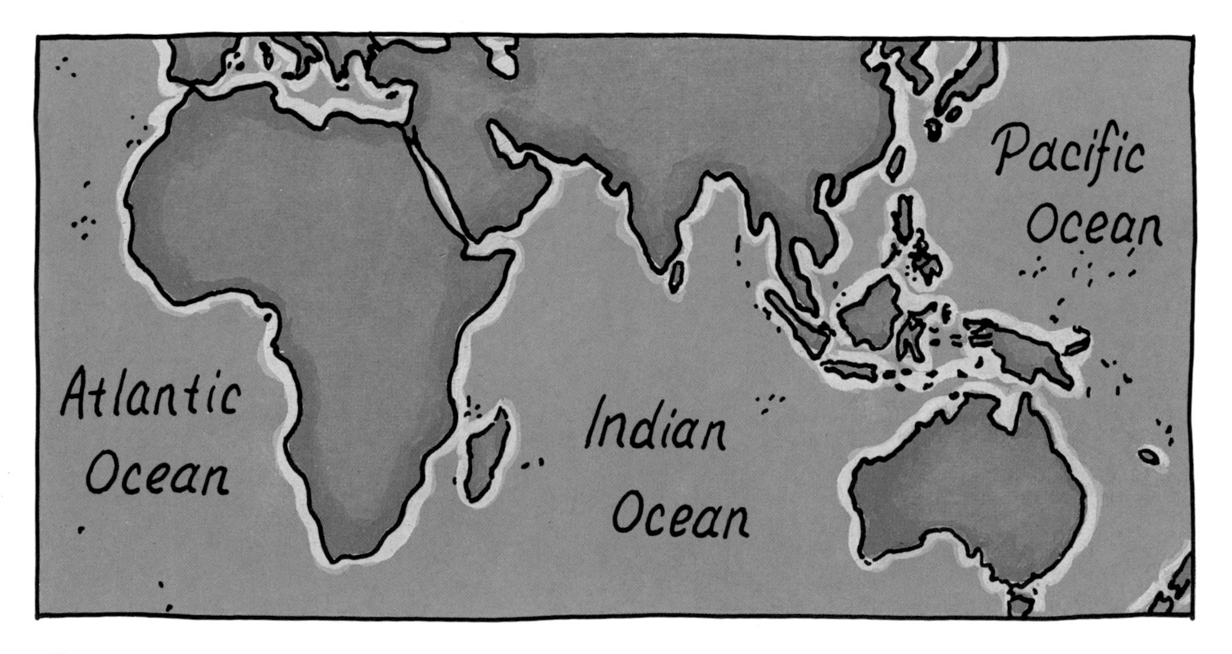

Ocean—(1) The entire body of salt water that covers nearly three-quarters of the earth's surface. (2) Any one of the five separate oceans: the Atlantic, Pacific, Indian, Arctic, or Antarctic.

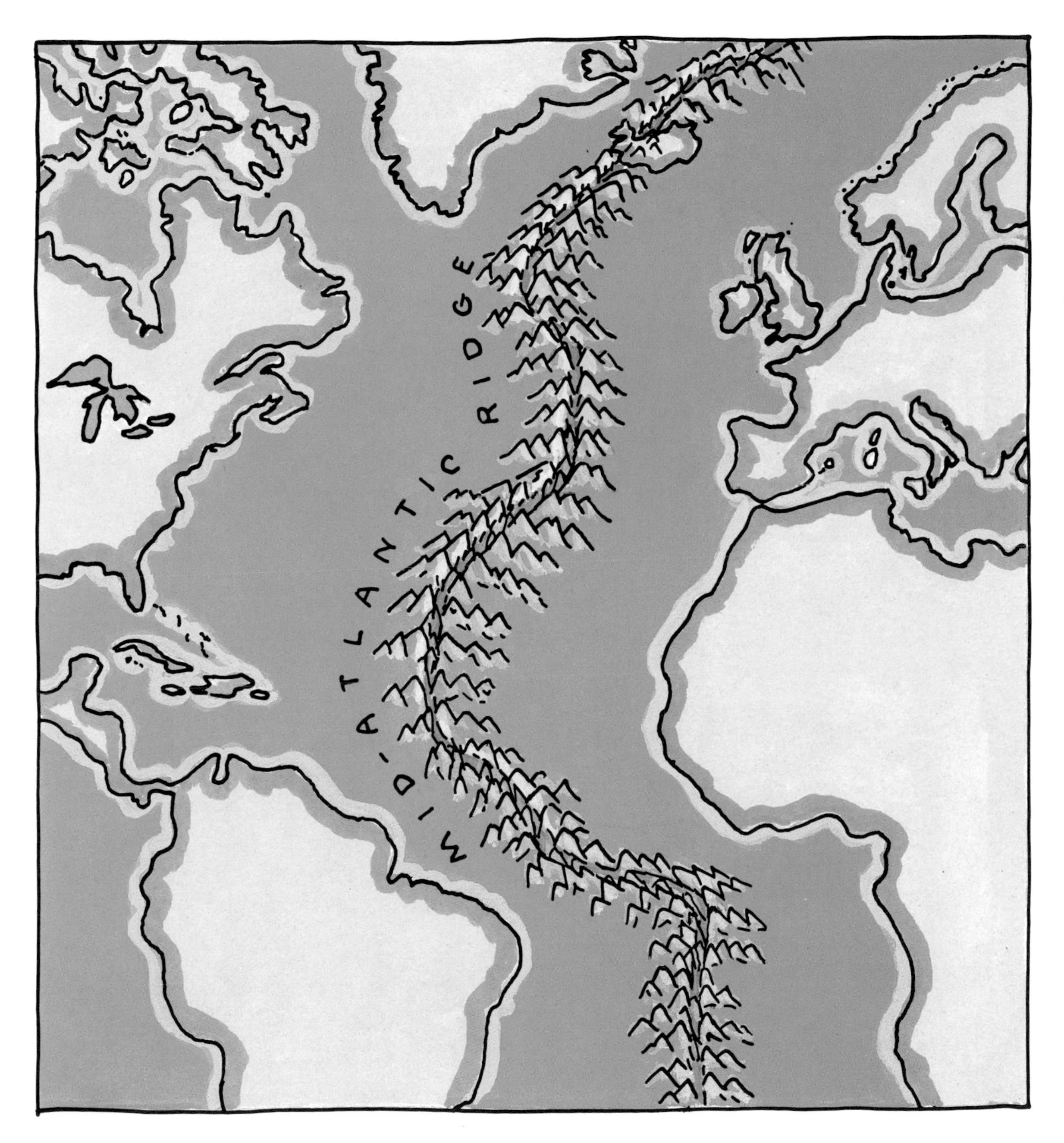

Ocean Ridge—a massive mountain range lying at the bottom of an ocean or sea. An **ocean trench** is a deep, narrow canyon in the ocean floor. There are more mountains and more canyons underwater than there are on dry land.

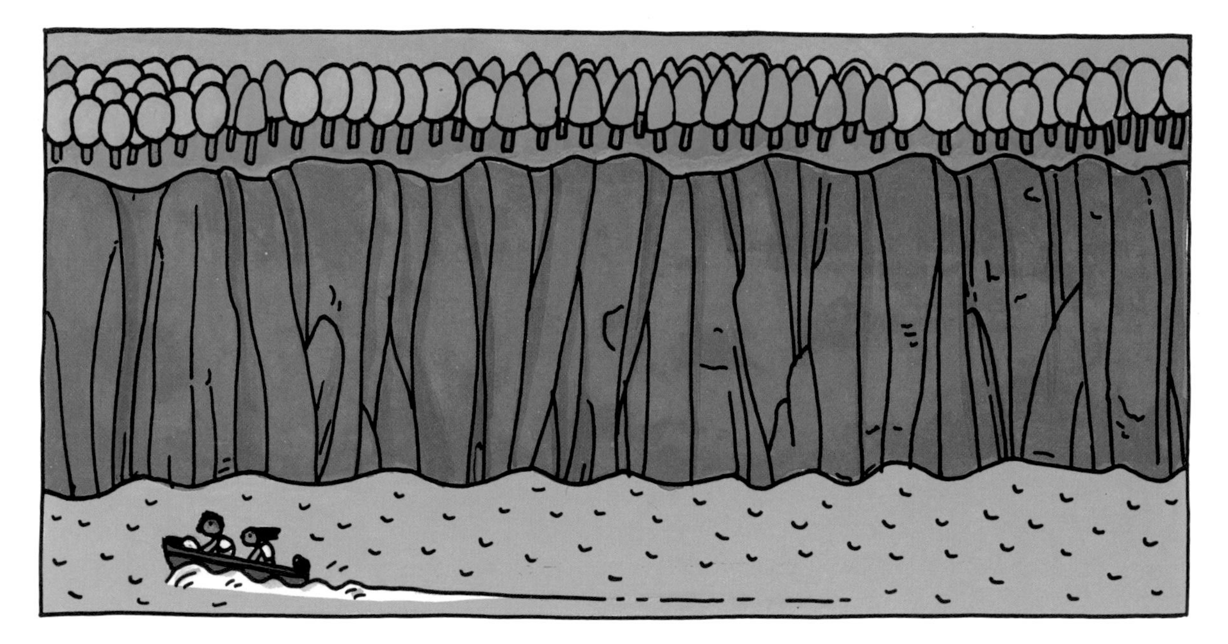

Palisade—a bold line of high, steep cliffs. A long palisade that joins two level areas of land is an **escarpment**.

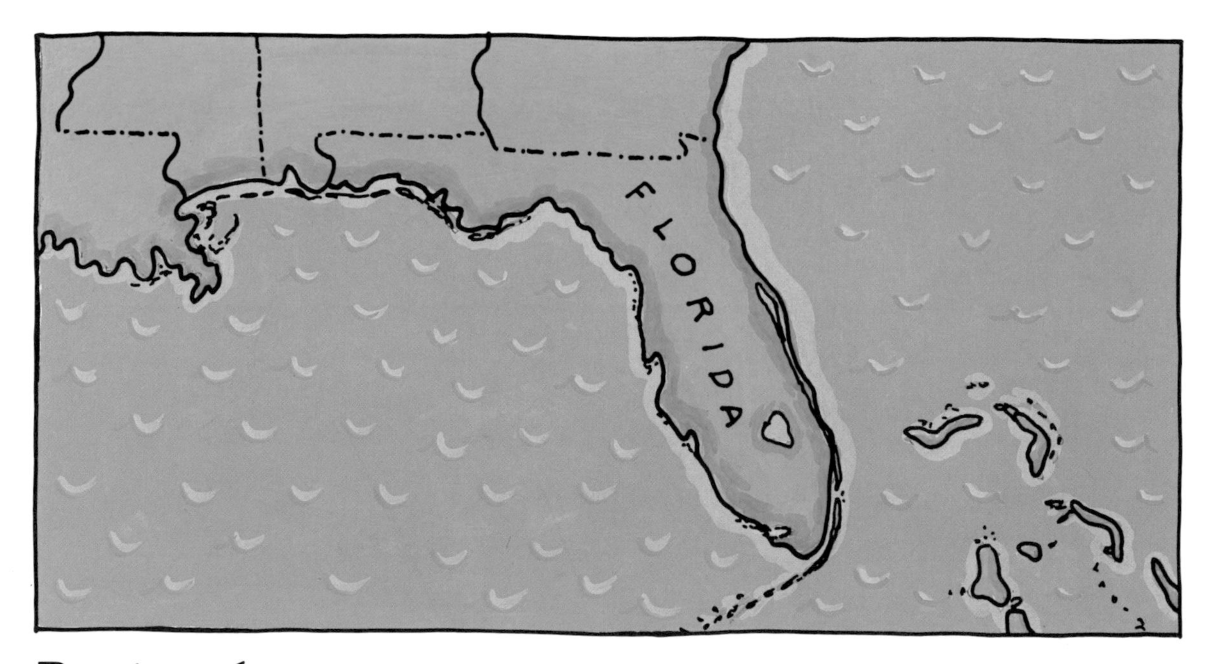

Peninsula—a large piece of land that juts far out into the water and is almost surrounded by water. Florida is a peninsula.

Plain—a broad region of flat or gently rolling, treeless land.

Plateau—a large highland plain that rises sharply above the surrounding land. Plateaus are also called **tablelands**.

Promontory or **Headland**—a high, prominent point on a rocky coastline. Promontories are ideal sites for lighthouses.

Rapids—a stretch of stream or river where the fast-moving current crashes against the rocks and boulders in its path. Seething, foaming rapids are sometimes called **white water**.

Reef—a narrow chain of rock, sand, or coral lurking just below or just above the water.

River—a long, large stream. Major rivers have many **tributary** streams and rivers flowing into them. The region drained by a great river and all its tributaries is called a **drainage basin** or **watershed**.

Sandbank or Sandbar—an underwater ridge of sand built up by tides and currents. Sandbanks and sandbars create areas of shallow water called **shoals**.

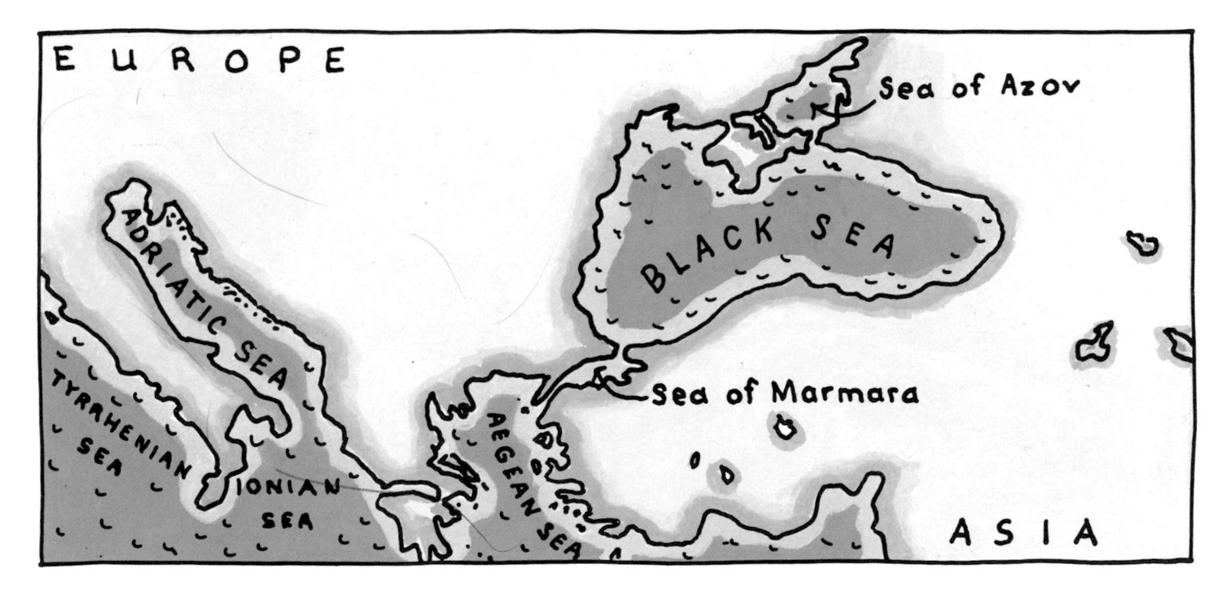

Sea—a large body of salt water that is smaller than an ocean. *Sea* and *ocean* are often used interchangeably to refer to great bodies of salt water.

Sea Cave—a hollow chamber eaten into a coastal cliff by the pounding power of crashing waves. **Sea arches** and **sea stacks** are also carved from these rocky cliffs.

Seamount—an underwater mountain. A tall seamount whose sharp, jagged peak is just below the surface of the ocean is a **pinnacle**. A seamount with a flat top is called a **guyot**.

Sound—a long, broad ocean inlet that is roughly parallel to the coast.

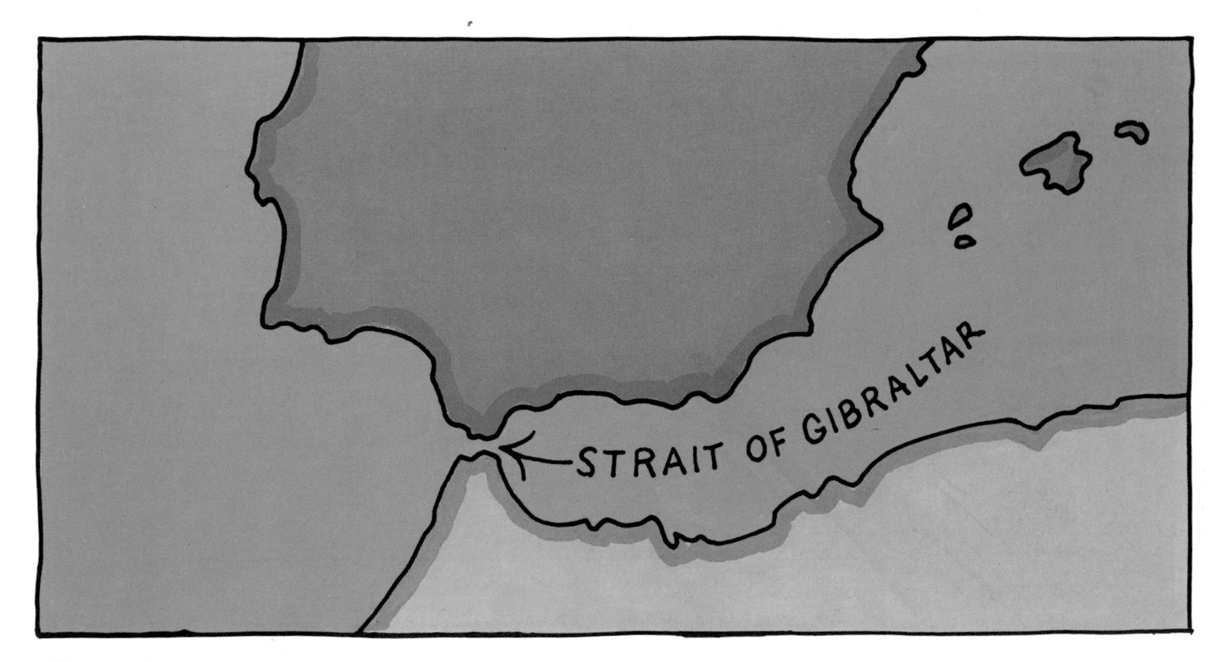

Strait—a narrow waterway that connects two larger bodies of water. Straits are also called **channels**, **passages**, and **narrows**.

Stream—a body of flowing water. A **brook** is a small stream, a **creek** is medium-sized, and a **river** is the largest of streams. The high sides along the edges of streams are called **banks**.

Swamp—a marsh with trees. Swamps usually contain more water and deeper water than marshes. Deep, dangerous pools of **quicksand** are sometimes found near swamps and marshes.

Tundra—a huge, treeless plain bordering the Arctic Ocean. **Alpine tundras** are found on mountain slopes at altitudes where trees cannot grow.

Valley—a gently sloping depression between hills or mountains. A stream flows along the floor of many valleys. Small valleys with creeks flowing through them are called **hollows**.

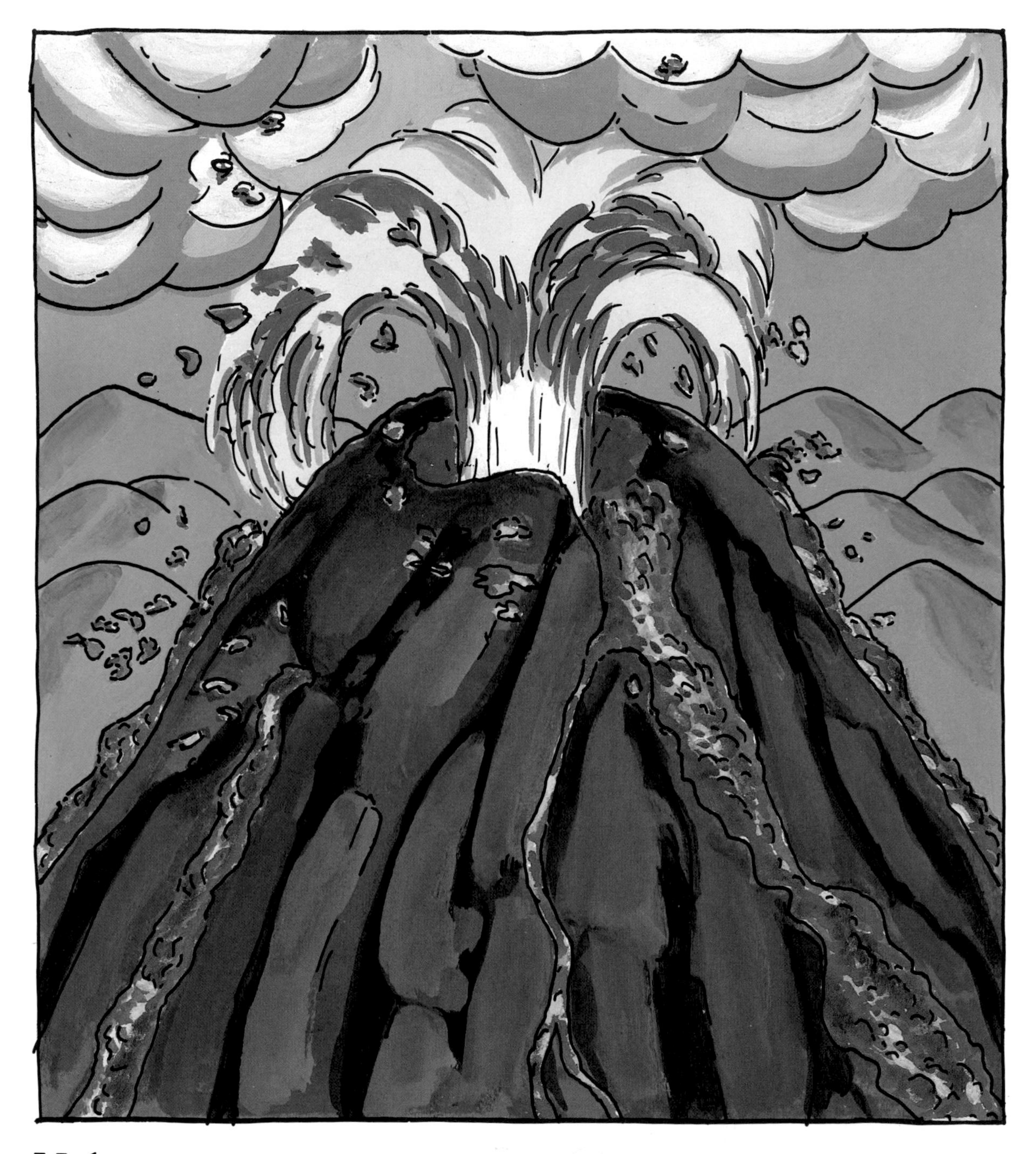

Volcano—an opening or vent in the earth's crust through which ashes, hot gases, and lava erupt. **Lava** is a fiery liquid formed of hot, melted rock. As lava cools, it often forms cone-shaped mountains.

Waterfall—a stream that flows over the edge of a cliff. There are two types of waterfalls.

Cataract—a large, dramatic waterfall that plunges down from a high, overhanging precipice.

Cascade—a small, splashing waterfall that tumbles down a mountainside in a series of steps.

cataract

cascade

Zone—a broad belt of climate and geography that encircles the earth. There are five zones on the earth.

Tropical or **torrid zone**—the hot, steamy region that lies just north and south of the equator.

Temperate zones—the two moderate regions that lie north of and south of the tropical zone. Each zone has hot summers, cold winters, and milder seasons in between.

Polar zones—the icy-cold regions at each pole. The northern polar zone, named the **Arctic**, is at the top of the earth. The southern zone, named the **Antarctic**, is at the bottom of the earth.

POLAR
Arctic Circle
TEMPERATE
Tropic of Cancer
TROPICAL
Equator
Tropic of Capricorn
TEMPERATE
Antarctic Circle
POLAR

ABOUT THE AUTHOR

Jack Knowlton was born in Florida. He is a free-lance writer living in New York City and is the author of MAPS & GLOBES, which was featured on *Reading Rainbow.*

ABOUT THE ARTIST

Harriett Wyatt Barton was born in Miami, Oklahoma, and now lives and works in New York City. She has illustrated a number of books for the Let's-Read-and-Find-Out Science Book series, including RAIN AND HAIL and NO MEASLES, NO MUMPS FOR ME.